CHILDREN'S THRIFT CLASSICS

Favorite Russian Fairy Tales

ARTHUR RANSOME

Illustrated by Simon Galkin

DOVER PUBLICATIONS, INC.
New York

DOVER CHILDREN'S THRIFT CLASSICS
THIS VOLUME EDITED BY: THOMAS CROFTS

Copyright

Published in Canada by General Publishing Company, Ltd., 30 Lesmill Road, Don Mills, Toronto, Ontario.
Published in the United Kingdom by Constable and Company, Ltd., 3 The Lanchesters, 162–164 Fulham Palace Road, London W6 9ER.

Bibliographical Note

Favorite Russian Fairy Tales, first published by Dover Publications, Inc. in 1995, reprints, in a slightly edited form, six stories from *Old Peter's Russian Tales* by Arthur Ransome, originally published by T. C. and E. C. Jack, Ltd., London, in 1916. The illustrations and introductory Note have been specially prepared for the present edition.

Library of Congress Cataloging-in-Publication Data

Ransome, Arthur, 1884–1967.
    Favorite Russian fairy tales / Arthur Ransome ; illustrated by Simon Galkin.
        p.   cm. — (Dover children's thrift classics)
    Reprints, in a slightly edited form, six stories from Old Peter's Russian tales originally published in London in 1916.
    Contents: Sadko — Frost — Baba Yaga — The little daughter of the snow — Alenoushka and her brother—The fire-bird, the horse of power, and Princess Vasilissa.
    ISBN 0–486–28632–0 (pbk.)
    1. Fairy tales—Russia. [1. Fairy tales. 2. Folklore—Russia.] I. Galkin, Simon, ill. II. Title. III. Series.
PZ8.R174Fav   1995   94-45619
398.2'0947—dc20   CIP
                                                            AC

Manufactured in the United States of America
Dover Publications, Inc., 31 East 2nd Street, Mineola, N.Y. 11501

Note

These six classic fairy tales transported children's imaginations in old Russia, and still do so today. They are filled with magic beasts, daring young men, beautiful maidens, wicked witches and, as might be expected, lots of snow.

In one of the most famous of these tales we are introduced to Baba Yaga, a fearsome witch whose legs are just bone and who has metal jaws and drives a mortar and pestle through the woods. Not surprisingly, she likes to eat children. On the other hand, she can also underestimate their cleverness. The composer Moussorgsky devoted one section of his *Pictures at an Exhibition* to Baba Yaga.

In another tale we catch sight of the magnificent fire-bird, whose feathers are made of gold. Rising at dawn, it sheds golden light over the forest as it flies. The glorious beauty of a single feather from the fire-bird changes forever the life of a young archer. The archer also rides a magic horse called a "horse of power" who can gallop mightily and give very good advice. Stravinsky's ballet *The Firebird* is based on this story.

The other Russian classics in this book include "Sadko" and "The Little Daughter of the Snow" (Rimsky-Korsakov wrote operas based on both of these), as well as "Frost" and "Alenoushka and Her Brother."

The author, Arthur Michell Ransome, lived from 1884 to 1967, and traveled from his native England to Russia, China and Egypt, among other places, collecting folk and fairy tales for his many children's books.

Contents

List of Illustrations

Sadko

IN NOVGOROD in the old days there was a young man—just a boy he was—the son of a rich merchant who had lost all his money and died. So Sadko was very poor. He had not a kopeck in the world, except what the people gave him when he played his dulcimer for their dancing. He had blue eyes and curling hair, and he was strong, and would have been merry; but it is dull work playing for other folk to dance, and Sadko dared not dance with any young girl, for he had no money to marry on, and he did not want to be chased away as a beggar. And the young women of Novgorod, they never looked at the handsome Sadko. No; they smiled with their bright eyes at the young men who danced with them, and if they ever spoke to Sadko, it was just to tell him sharply to keep the music going or to play faster.

So Sadko lived alone with his dulcimer, and made do with half a loaf when he could not get a whole, and with crust when he had no crumb. He did not mind so very much what came to him, so long as he could play his dulcimer and walk along the banks of the little river Volkhov that flows by Novgorod, or on the shores of the lake, making music for himself, and seeing the pale mists rise over the water, and dawn or sunset across the shining river.

"There is no girl in all Novgorod as pretty as my little river," he used to say, and night after night he would sit by the banks of the river or on the shores of the lake, playing the dulcimer and singing to himself.

Sometimes he helped the fishermen on the lake, and they would give him a little fish for his supper in payment for his strong young arms.

And it happened that one evening the fishermen asked him to watch their nets for them on the shore, while they went off to take their fish to sell them in the square at Novgorod.

Sadko sat on the shore, on a rock, and played his dulcimer and sang. Very sweetly he sang of the fair lake and the lovely river—the little river that he thought prettier than all the girls of Novgorod. And while he was singing he saw a whirlpool in the lake, little waves flying from it across the water, and in the middle a hollow down into the water. And in the hollow he saw the head of a great man with blue hair and a gold crown. He knew that the huge man was the Tzar of the Sea. And the man came nearer, walking up out of the depths of the lake—a huge, great man, a very giant, with blue hair falling to his waist over his broad shoulders. The little waves ran from him in all directions as he came striding up out of the water.

Sadko did not know whether to run or stay; but the Tzar of the Sea called out to him in a great voice like wind and water in a storm, —

"Sadko of Novgorod, you have played and sung many days by the side of this lake and on the banks of the little river Volkhov. My daughters love your music, and it has pleased me too. Throw out a net into the water, and draw it in, and the waters will pay you for your singing. And if you are satisfied with the payment, you must come and play to us down in the green palace of the sea."

With that the Tzar of the Sea went down again into the waters of the lake. The waves closed over him with a roar, and presently the lake was as smooth and calm as it had ever been.

Sadko thought, and said to himself: "Well, there is no harm done in casting out a net." So he threw a net out into the lake.

He sat down again and played on his dulcimer and sang, and when he had finished his singing the dusk had fallen and the moon shone over the lake. He put down his dulcimer and took hold of the ropes of the net, and began to draw it up out of the silver water. Easily the ropes came, and the net, dripping and glittering in the moonlight.

"I was dreaming," said Sadko; "I was asleep when I saw the Tzar of the Sea, and there is nothing in the net at all."

And then, just as the last of the net was coming ashore, he saw something in it, square and dark. He dragged it out, and found it was a coffer. He opened the coffer, and it was full of precious stones—green, red, gold—gleaming in the light of the moon. Diamonds shone there like little bundles of sharp knives.

"There can be no harm in taking these stones," says Sadko, "whether I dreamed or not."

He took the coffer on his shoulder, and bent under the weight of it, strong though he was. He put it in a safe place. All night he sat and watched by the nets, and played and sang, and planned what he would do.

In the morning the fishermen came, laughing and merry after their night in Novgorod, and they gave him a little fish for watching their nets; and he made a fire on the shore, and cooked it and ate it as he used to do.

"And that is my last meal as a poor man," says Sadko. "Ah me! who knows if I shall be happier?"

Then he set the coffer on his shoulder and tramped away for Novgorod.

"Who is that?" they asked at the gates.

"Only Sadko the dulcimer player," he replied.

"Turned porter?" said they.

"One trade is as good as another," said Sadko, and he walked into the city. He sold a few of the stones, two at a time, and with what he got for them he set up a booth in the market. Small things led to great, and he was soon one of the richest traders in Novgorod.

And now there was not a girl in the town who could look too sweetly at Sadko. "He has golden hair," says one. "Blue eyes like the sea," says another. "He could lift the world on his shoulders," says a third. A little money, you see, opens everybody's eyes.

But Sadko was not changed by his good fortune. Still he walked and played by the little river Volkhov. When work was done and the traders gone, Sadko would take his dulcimer and play and sing on the banks of the river. And still he said, "There is no girl in all Novgorod as pretty as my little river." Every time he came back from his long voyages—for he was trading far and near, like the greatest of merchants—he went at once to the banks of the river to see how his sweetheart fared. And always he brought some little present for her and threw it into the waves.

For twelve years he lived unmarried in Novgorod, and every year made voyages, buying and selling, and always growing richer and richer. Many were the mothers in Novgorod who would have liked to see him married to their daughters. Many were the pillows that were wet with the tears of the young girls, as they thought of the blue eyes of Sadko and his golden hair.

And then, in the twelfth year since he walked into Novgorod with the coffer on his shoulder, he was sailing in a ship on the Caspian Sea, far, far away. For many days the ship sailed on, and Sadko sat on deck and played his dulcimer and sang of Novgorod and of the little river Volkhov that flows under the walls of the town. Blue was the Caspian Sea, and the waves were like furrows in a field, long lines of white under the steady wind, while the sails swelled and the ship shot over the water.

And suddenly the ship stopped.

In the middle of the sea, far from land, the ship stopped and trembled in the waves, as if she were held by a big hand.

"We are aground!" cry the sailors; and the captain, the great one, tells them to take soundings. Seventy fathoms by the bow it was, and seventy fathoms by the stern.

"We are not aground," says the captain, "unless there is a rock sticking up like a needle in the middle of the Caspian Sea!"

"There is magic in this," say the sailors.

"Hoist more sail," says the captain; and up go the white sails, swelling out in the wind, while the masts bend and creak. But still the ship lay shivering and did not move, out there in the middle of the sea.

"Hoist more sail yet," says the captain; and up go the white sails, swelling and tugging, while the masts creak and groan. But still the ship lay there shivering and did not move.

"There is an unlucky one aboard," says an old sailor. "We must draw lots and find him, and throw him overboard into the sea."

The other sailors agreed to this. And still Sadko sat, and played his dulcimer and sang.

The sailors cut pieces of string, all of a length, as many as there were souls in the ship, and one of those strings they cut in half. Then they made them into a bundle, and each man plucked one string. And Sadko stopped his playing for a moment to pluck a string, and his was the string that had been cut in half.

"Magician, sorcerer, unclean one!" shouted the sailors.

"Not so," said Sadko. "I remember now an old promise I made, and I keep it willingly."

He took his dulcimer in his hand, and leapt from the ship into the blue Caspian Sea. The waves had scarcely closed over his head before the ship shot forward again, and flew over the waves like a swan's feather, and came in the end safely to her harbour.

Sadko dropped into the waves, and the waves closed over him. Down he sank, like a pebble thrown into a pool, down and down. First the water was blue, then green, and strange fish with goggle eyes and golden fins swam round him as he sank. He came at last to the bottom of the sea.

And there, on the bottom of the sea, was a palace built of green wood. Yes, all the timbers of all the ships that have been wrecked in all the seas of the world are in that palace, and they are all green, and cunningly fitted together, so that the palace is worth a ten days' journey only to see it. And in front of the palace Sadko saw two big kobbly sturgeons, each a hundred and fifty feet long, lashing their tails and guarding the gates. Now, sturgeons are the oldest of all fish, and these were the oldest of all sturgeons.

Sadko walked between the sturgeons and through the gates of the palace. Inside there was a great hall, and the Tzar of the Sea lay resting in the hall, with his gold crown on his head and his blue hair floating round him in the water, and his great body covered with scales lying along the hall. The Tzar of the Sea filled the hall—and there is room in that hall for a village. And there were fish swimming this way and that in and out of the windows.

"Ah, Sadko," says the Tzar of the Sea, "you took what the sea gave you, but you have been a long time in coming to sing in the palaces of the sea. Twelve years I have lain here waiting for you."

"Great Tzar, forgive," says Sadko.

"Sing now," says the Tzar of the Sea, and his voice was like the beating of waves.

And Sadko played on his dulcimer and sang.

He sang of Novgorod and of the little river Volkhov which he loved. It was in his song that none of the girls of Novgorod were as pretty as the little river. And there was the sound of wind over the lake in his song, the sound of ripples under the prow of a boat, the sound of ripples on the shore, the sound of the river flowing past the tall reeds, the whispering sound of the river at night. And all the time he played cunningly on the dulcimer. The girls of Novgorod had never danced to so sweet a tune when in the old days Sadko played his dulcimer to earn kopecks and crusts of bread.

Never had the Tzar of the Sea heard such music.

"I would dance," said the Tzar of the Sea, and he stood up like a tall tree in the hall.

"Play on," said the Tzar of the Sea, and he strode through the gates. The sturgeons guarding the gates stirred the water with their tails.

And if the Tzar of the Sea was huge in the hall, he was huger still when he stood outside on the bottom of the sea. He grew taller and taller, towering like a mountain. His feet were like small hills. His

blue hair hung down to his waist, and he was covered with green scales. And he began to dance on
the bottom of the sea.

Great was that dancing. The sea boiled, and
ships went down. The waves rolled as big as
houses. The sea overflowed its shores, and whole
towns were under water as the Tzar danced mightily on the bottom of the sea. Hither and thither
rushed the waves, and the very earth shook at the
dancing of that tremendous Tzar.

He danced till he was tired, and then he came
back to the palace of green wood, and passed the
sturgeons, and shrank into himself and came
through the gates into the hall, where Sadko still
played on his dulcimer and sang.

"You have played well and given me pleasure,"
says the Tzar of the Sea. "I have thirty daughters,
and you shall choose one and marry her, and be a
Prince of the Sea."

"Better than all maidens I love my little river,"
says Sadko; and the Tzar of the Sea laughed and
threw his head back, with his blue hair floating all
over the hall.

And then there came in the thirty daughters of the
Tzar of the Sea. Beautiful they were, lovely, and
graceful; but twenty-nine of them passed by, and
Sadko fingered his dulcimer and thought of his little river.

There came in the thirtieth, and Sadko cried out

He began to dance on the bottom of the sea.

aloud. "Here is the only maiden in the world as pretty as my little river!" says he. And she looked at him with eyes that shone like stars reflected in the river. Her hair was dark, like the river at night. She laughed, and her voice was like the flowing of the river.

"And what is the name of your little river?" says the Tzar.

"It is the little river Volkhov that flows by Novgorod," says Sadko; "but your daughter is as fair as the little river, and I would gladly marry her if she will have me."

"It is a strange thing," says the Tzar, "but Volkhov is the name of my youngest daughter."

He put Sadko's hand in the hand of his youngest daughter, and they kissed each other. And as they kissed, Sadko saw a necklace round her neck, and knew it for one he had thrown into the river as a present for his sweetheart.

She smiled, and "Come!" says she, and took him away to a palace of her own, and showed him a coffer; and in that coffer were bracelets and rings and earrings—all the gifts that he had thrown into the river.

And Sadko laughed for joy, and kissed the youngest daughter of the Tzar of the Sea, and she kissed him back.

"O my little river!" says he; "there is no girl in all the world but thou as pretty as my little river."

Well, they were married, and the Tzar of the Sea

laughed at the wedding feast till the palace shook and the fish swam off in all directions.

And after the feast Sadko and his bride went off together to her palace. And before they slept she kissed him very tenderly, and she said, —

"O Sadko, you will not forget me? You will play to me sometimes, and sing?"

"I shall never lose sight of you, my pretty one," says he; "and as for music, I will sing and play all the day long."

"That's as may be," says she, and they fell asleep.

And in the middle of the night Sadko happened to turn in bed, and he touched the Princess with his left foot, and she was cold, cold, cold as ice in January. And with that touch of cold he woke, and he was lying under the walls of Novgorod, with his dulcimer in his hand, and one of his feet was in the little river Volkhov, and the moon was shining.

After that some say he went into the town, and lived on alone until he died. Others say that he took his dulcimer and swam out into the middle of the river, and sank under water again, looking for his little Princess. They say he found her, and lives still in the green palaces of the bottom of the sea; and when there is a big storm, you may know that Sadko is playing on his dulcimer and singing, and that the Tzar of the Sea is dancing his tremendous dance down there, on the bottom, under the waves.

Frost

ONCE UPON a time there were an old man and an old woman. Now the old woman was the old man's second wife. His first wife had died, and had left him with a little daughter: Martha she was called. Then he married again, and God gave him a cross wife, and with her two more daughters, and they were very different from the first.

The old woman loved her own daughters, and gave them red kisel jelly every day, and honey too, as much as they could put into their greedy little mouths. But poor little Martha, the eldest, she got only what the others left. When they were cross they threw away what they left, and then she got nothing at all.

The children grew older, and the stepmother made Martha do all the work of the house. She had to fetch the wood for the stove, and light it and keep it burning. She had to draw the water for her sisters to wash their hands in. She had to make the clothes, and wash them and mend them. She had to cook the dinner, and clean the dishes after the others had done before having a bite for herself.

For all that the stepmother was never satisfied, and was for ever shouting at her: "Look, the kettle is in the wrong place;" "There is dust on the floor;" "There is a spot on the tablecloth;" or, "The spoons are not clean, you stupid, ugly, idle hussy." But Martha was not idle. She worked all day long, and got up before the sun, while her sisters never stirred from their beds till it was time for dinner. And she was not stupid. She always had a song on her lips, except when her stepmother had beaten her. And as for being ugly, she was the prettiest little girl in the village.

Her father saw all this, but he could not do anything, for the old woman was mistress at home, and he was terribly afraid of her. And as for the daughters, they saw how their mother treated Martha, and they did the same. They were always complaining and getting her into trouble. It was a pleasure to them to see the tears on her pretty cheeks.

Well, time went on, and the little girl grew up, and the daughters of the stepmother were as ugly as could be. Their eyes were always cross, and their mouths were always complaining. Their mother saw that no one would want to marry either of them while there was Martha about the house, with her bright eyes and her songs and her kindness to everybody.

So she thought of a way to get rid of her step-daughter, and a cruel way it was.

"See here, old man," says she, "it is high time Martha was married, and I have a bridegroom in mind for her. To-morrow morning you must harness the old mare to the sledge, and put a bit of food together and be ready to start early, as I'd like to see you back before night."

To Martha she said: "To-morrow you must pack your things in a box, and put on your best dress to show yourself to your betrothed."

"Who is he?" asked Martha with red cheeks.

"You will know when you see him," said the step-mother.

All that night Martha hardly slept. She could hardly believe that she was really going to escape from the old woman at last, and have a hut of her own, where there would be no one to scold her. She wondered who the young man was. She hoped he was Fedor Ivanovitch, who had such kind eyes, and such nimble fingers on the balalaika, and such a merry way of flinging out his heels when he danced the Russian dance. But although he always smiled at her when they met, she felt she hardly dared to hope that it was he. Early in the morning she got up and said her prayers to God, put the whole hut in order, and packed her things into a little box. That was easy, because she had such few things. It was the other daughters who had new dresses. Any old thing was good enough for Martha. But she put on her best blue dress, and there she was, as pretty a little maid as ever walked under the birch trees in spring.

The old man harnessed the mare to the sledge and brought it to the door. The snow was very deep and frozen hard, and the wind peeled the skin from his ears before he covered them with the flaps of his fur hat.

"Sit down at the table and have a bite before you go," says the old woman.

The old man sat down, and his daughter with him, and drank a glass of tea and ate some black bread. And the old woman put some cabbage soup, left from the day before, in a saucer, and said to Martha, "Eat this, my little pigeon, and get ready for the road." But when she said "my little pigeon," she did not smile with her eyes, but only with her cruel mouth, and Martha was afraid. The old woman whispered to the old man: "I have a word for you, old fellow. You will take Martha to her betrothed, and I'll tell you the way. You go straight along, and then take the road to the right into the forest . . . you know . . . straight to the big fir tree that stands on a hillock, and there you will give Martha to her betrothed and leave her. He will be waiting for her, and his name is Frost."

The old man stared, opened his mouth, and stopped eating. The little maid, who had heard the last words, began to cry.

"Now, what are you whimpering about?" screamed the old woman. "Frost is a rich bridegroom and a handsome one. See how much he owns. All the pines and firs are his, and the birch trees. Any one would envy his possessions, and he himself is a very bogatir,* a man of strength and power."

The old man trembled, and said nothing in reply. And Martha went on crying quietly, though she tried to stop her tears. The old man packed up what was left of the black bread, told Martha to put on her sheepskin coat, set her in the sledge and climbed in, and drove off along the white, frozen road.

The road was long and the country open, and the wind grew colder and colder, while the frozen snow blew up from under the hoofs of the mare and spattered the sledge with white patches. The tale is soon told, but it takes time to happen, and the sledge was white all over long before they turned off into the forest.

They came in the end deep into the forest, and left the road, and over the deep snow through the trees to the great fir. There the old man stopped, told his daughter to get out of the sledge, set her little box under the fir, and said, "Wait here for your bridegroom, and when he comes be sure to receive him with kind words." Then he turned the mare round and drove home, with the tears running from

* The bogatirs were strong men, heroes of old Russia.

his eyes and freezing on his cheeks before they had had time to reach his beard.

The little maid sat and trembled. Her sheepskin coat was worn through, and in her blue bridal dress she sat, while fits of shivering shook her whole body. She wanted to run away; but she had not strength to move, or even to keep her little white teeth from chattering between her frozen lips.

Suddenly, not far away, she heard Frost crackling among the fir trees. He was leaping from tree to tree, crackling as he came.

He leapt at last into the great fir tree, under which the little maid was sitting. He crackled in the top of the tree, and then called down out of the topmost branches,—

"Are you warm, little maid?"

"Warm, warm, little Father Frost."

Frost laughed, and came a little lower in the tree and crackled and crackled louder than before. Then he asked,—

"Are you still warm, little maid? Are you warm, little red cheeks?"

The little maid could hardly speak. She was nearly dead, but she answered,—

"Warm, dear Frost; warm, little father."

Frost climbed lower in the tree, and crackled louder than ever, and asked,—

"Are you still warm, little maid? Are you warm, little red cheeks? Are you warm, little paws?"

The little maid was benumbed all over, but she whispered so that Frost could just hear her,—

"Warm, little pigeon, warm, dear Frost."

And Frost was sorry for her, leapt down with a tremendous crackle and a scattering of frozen snow, wrapped the little maid up in rich furs, and covered her with warm blankets.

In the morning the old woman said to her husband, "Drive off now to the forest, and wake the young couple."

The old man wept when he thought of his little daughter, for he was sure that he would find her dead. He harnessed the mare, and drove off through the snow. He came to the tree, and heard his little daughter singing merrily, while Frost crackled and laughed. There she was, alive and warm, with a good fur cloak about her shoulders, a rich veil, costly blankets round her feet, and a box full of splendid presents.

The old man did not say a word. He was too surprised. He just sat in the sledge staring, while the little maid lifted her box and the box of presents, set them in the sledge, climbed in, and sat down beside him.

They came home, and the little maid, Martha, fell at the feet of her stepmother. The old woman nearly went off her head with rage when she saw her alive, with her fur cloak and rich veil, and the box of splendid presents fit for the daughter of a prince.

There she was, alive and warm, with a good fur cloak about her shoulders.

"Ah, you chit," she cried, "you won't get round me like that!"

And she would not say another word to the little maid, but went about all day long biting her nails and thinking what to do.

At night she said to the old man, —

"You must take my daughters, too, to that bridegroom in the forest. He will give them better gifts than these."

Things take time to happen, but the tale is quickly told. Early next morning the old woman woke her daughters, fed them with good food, dressed them like brides, hustled the old man, made him put clean hay in the sledge and warm blankets, and sent them off to the forest.

The old man did as he was bid—drove to the big fir tree, set the boxes under the tree, lifted out the stepdaughters and set them on the boxes side by side, and drove back home.

They were warmly dressed, these two, and well fed, and at first, as they sat there, they did not think about the cold.

"I can't think what put it into mother's head to marry us both at once," said the first, "and to send us here to be married. As if there were not enough young men in the village. Who can tell what sort of fellows we shall meet here!"

Then they began to quarrel.

"Well," says one of them, "I'm beginning to get the cold shivers. If our fated ones do not come soon, we shall perish of cold."

"It's a flat lie to say that bridegrooms get ready early. It's already dinner-time."

"What if only one comes?"

"You'll have to come another time."

"You think he'll look at you?"

"Well, he won't take you, anyhow."

"Of course he'll take me."

"Take you first! It's enough to make any one laugh!"

They began to fight and scratch each other, so that their cloaks fell open and the cold entered their bosoms.

Frost, crackling among the trees, laughing to himself, froze the hands of the two quarrelling girls, and they hid their hands in the sleeves of their fur coats and shivered, and went on scolding and jeering at each other.

"Oh, you ugly mug, dirty nose! What sort of a housekeeper will you make?"

"And what about you, boasting one? You know nothing but how to gad about and lick your own face. We'll soon see which of us he'll take."

And the two girls went on wrangling and wrangling till they began to freeze in good earnest.

Suddenly they cried out together,—

"Devil take these bridegrooms for being so long in coming! You have turned blue all over."

And together they replied, shivering,—

"No bluer than yourself, tooth-chatterer."

And Frost, not so far away, crackled and laughed, and leapt from fir tree to fir tree, crackling as he came.

The girls heard that some one was coming through the forest.

"Listen! there's some one coming. Yes, and with bells on his sledge!"

"Shut up, you chit! I can't hear, and the frost is taking the skin off me."

They began blowing on their fingers.

And Frost came nearer and nearer, crackling, laughing, talking to himself. Nearer and nearer he came, leaping from tree-top to tree-top, till at last he leapt into the great fir under which the two girls were sitting and quarrelling.

He leant down, looking through the branches, and asked,—

"Are you warm, maidens? Are you warm, little red cheeks? Are you warm, little pigeons?"

"Ugh, Frost, the cold is hurting us. We are frozen. We are waiting for our bridegrooms, but the cursed fellows have not turned up."

Frost came a little lower in the tree, and crackled louder and swifter.

"Are you warm, maidens? Are you warm, my little red cheeks?"

"Go to the devil!" they cried out. "Are you blind? Our hands and feet are frozen!"

Frost came still lower in the branches, and cracked and crackled louder than ever.

"Are you warm, maidens?" he asked.

"Into the pit with you, with all the fiends," the girls screamed at him, "you ugly, wretched fellow!" . . . And as they were cursing at him their bad words died on their lips, for the two girls, the cross children of the cruel stepmother, were frozen stiff where they sat.

Frost hung from the lowest branches of the tree, swaying and crackling while he looked at the anger frozen on their faces. Then he climbed swiftly up again, and crackling and cracking, chuckling to himself, he went off, leaping from fir tree to fir tree, this way and that through the white, frozen forest.

In the morning the old woman says to her husband,—

"Now then, old man, harness the mare to the sledge, and put new hay in the sledge to be warm for my little ones, and lay fresh rushes on the hay to be soft for them; and take warm rugs with you, for maybe they will be cold, even in their furs. And look sharp about it, and don't keep them waiting. The frost is hard this morning, and it was harder in the night."

The old man had not time to eat even a mouthful of black bread before she had driven him out into the snow. He put hay and rushes and soft blankets in the sledge, and harnessed the mare, and went off to the forest. He came to the great fir, and found the two girls sitting under it dead, with their anger still to be seen on their frozen, ugly faces.

He picked them up, first one and then the other, and put them in the rushes and the warm hay, covered them with the blankets, and drove home.

The old woman saw him coming, far away, over the shining snow. She ran to meet him, and shouted out, —

"Where are the little ones?"

"In the sledge."

She snatched off the blankets and pulled aside the rushes, and found the bodies of her two cross daughters.

Instantly she flew at the old man in a storm of rage. "What have you done to my children, my little red cherries, my little pigeons? I will kill you with the oven fork! I will break your head with the poker!"

The old man listened till she was out of breath and could not say another word. That is the only wise thing to do when somebody is in a scolding rage. And as soon as she had no breath left with which to answer him, he said, —

"My little daughter got riches for soft words, but yours were always rough of the tongue. And it's not my fault, anyhow, for you yourself sent them into the forest."

Well, at last the old woman got her breath again, and scolded away till she was tired out. But in the end she made her peace with the old man, and they lived together as quietly as could be expected.

As for Martha, Fedor Ivanovitch sought her in marriage, as he had meant to do all along—yes, and married her; and pretty she looked in the furs that Frost had given her. And she had the prettiest children that ever were seen—yes, and the best behaved. For if ever they thought of being naughty, the old grandfather told them the story of crackling Frost, and how kind words won kindness, and cross words cold treatment.

Baba Yaga

ONCE UPON a time there was a widowed old man who lived alone in a hut with his little daughter. Very merry they were together, and they used to smile at each other over a table just piled with bread and jam. Everything went well, until the old man took it into his head to marry again.

Yes, the old man became foolish in the years of his old age, and he took another wife. And so the poor little girl had a stepmother. And after that everything changed. There was no more bread and jam on the table, and no more playing bo-peep, first this side of the samovar and then that, as she sat with her father at tea. It was worse than that, for she never did sit at tea. The stepmother said that everything that went wrong was the little girl's fault. And the old man believed his new wife, and so there were no more kind words for his little daughter. Day after day the stepmother used to say that the little girl was too naughty to sit at table. And then she would throw her a crust and tell her to get out of the hut and go and eat it somewhere else.

29

And the poor little girl used to go away by herself into the shed in the yard, and wet the dry crust with her tears, and eat it all alone. Ah me! she often wept for the old days, and she often wept at the thought of the days that were to come.

Mostly she wept because she was all alone, until one day she found a little friend in the shed. She was hunched up in a corner of the shed, eating her crust and crying bitterly, when she heard a little noise. It was like this: scratch—scratch. It was just that, a little gray mouse who lived in a hole.

Out he came, his little pointed nose and his long whiskers, his little round ears and his bright eyes. Out came his little humpy body and his long tail. And then he sat up on his hind legs, and curled his tail twice round himself and looked at the little girl.

The little girl, who had a kind heart, forgot all her sorrows, and took a scrap of her crust and threw it to the little mouse. The mouseykin nibbled and nibbled, and there, it was gone, and he was looking for another. She gave him another bit, and presently that was gone, and another and another, until there was no crust left for the little girl. Well, she didn't mind that. You see, she was so happy seeing the little mouse nibbling and nibbling.

When the crust was done the mouseykin looks up at her with his little bright eyes, and "Thank you," he says, in a little squeaky voice. "Thank you," he says; "you are a kind little girl, and I am only a mouse, and I've eaten all your crust. But there is one thing I can do for you, and that is to tell you to take care. The old woman in the hut (and that was the cruel stepmother) is own sister to Baba Yaga, the bony-legged, the witch. So if ever she sends you on a message to your aunt, you come and tell me. For Baba Yaga would eat you soon enough with her iron teeth if you did not know what to do."

"Oh, thank you," said the little girl; and just then she heard the stepmother calling to her to come in and clean up the tea things, and tidy the house, and brush out the floor, and clean everybody's boots.

So off she had to go.

When she went in she had a good look at her stepmother, and sure enough she had a long nose, and she was as bony as a fish with all the flesh picked off, and the little girl thought of Baba Yaga and shivered, though she did not feel so bad when she remembered the mouseykin out there in the shed in the yard.

The very next morning it happened. The old man went off to pay a visit to some friends of his in the next village. And as soon as the old man was out of sight the wicked stepmother called the little girl.

"You are to go to-day to your dear little aunt in the forest," says she, "and ask her for a needle and thread to mend a shirt."

"But here is a needle and thread," says the little girl.

"Hold your tongue," says the stepmother, and she gnashes her teeth, and they make a noise like clattering tongs. "Hold your tongue," she says. "Didn't I tell you you are to go to-day to your dear little aunt to ask for a needle and thread to mend a shirt?"

"How shall I find her?" says the little girl, nearly ready to cry, for she knew that her aunt was Baba Yaga, the bony-legged, the witch.

The stepmother took hold of the little girl's nose and pinched it.

"That is your nose," she says. "Can you feel it?"

"Yes," says the poor little girl.

"You must go along the road into the forest till you come to a fallen tree; then you must turn to your left, and then follow your nose and you will find her," says the stepmother. "Now, be off with you, lazy one. Here is some food for you to eat by the way." She gave the little girl a bundle wrapped up in a towel.

The little girl wanted to go into the shed to tell the mouseykin she was going to Baba Yaga, and to ask what she should do. But she looked back, and there was the stepmother at the door watching her. So she had to go straight on.

She walked along the road through the forest till she came to the fallen tree. Then she turned to the

left. Her nose was still hurting where the stepmother had pinched it, so she knew she had to go
straight ahead. She was just setting out when she
heard a little noise under the fallen tree.

"Scratch—scratch."

And out jumped the little mouse, and sat up in
the road in front of her.

"O mouseykin, mouseykin," says the little girl,
"my stepmother has sent me to her sister. And that
is Baba Yaga, the bony-legged, the witch, and I do
not know what to do."

"It will not be difficult," says the little mouse,
"because of your kind heart. Take all the things you
find in the road, and do with them what you like.
Then you will escape from Baba Yaga, and everything will be well."

"Are you hungry, mouseykin?" said the little girl.

"I could nibble, I think," says the little mouse.

The little girl unfastened the towel, and there was
nothing in it but stones. That was what the stepmother had given the little girl to eat by the way.

"Oh, I'm so sorry," says the little girl. "There's
nothing for you to eat."

"Isn't there?" said mouseykin, and as she looked
at them the little girl saw the stones turn to bread
and jam. The little girl sat down on the fallen tree,
and the little mouse sat beside her, and they ate
bread and jam until they were not hungry any more.

"Keep the towel," says the little mouse; "I think it

will be useful. And remember what I said about the things you find on the way. And now good-bye," says he.

"Good-bye," says the little girl, and runs along.

As she was running along she found a nice new handkerchief lying in the road. She picked it up and took it with her. Then she found a little bottle of oil. She picked it up and took it with her. Then she found some scraps of meat.

"Perhaps I'd better take them too," she said; and she took them.

Then she found a gay blue ribbon, and she took that. Then she found a little loaf of good bread, and she took that too.

"I daresay somebody will like it," she said.

And then she came to the hut of Baba Yaga, the bony-legged, the witch. There was a high fence round it with big gates. When she pushed them open they squeaked miserably, as if it hurt them to move. The little girl was sorry for them.

"How lucky," she says, "that I picked up the bottle of oil!" and she poured the oil into the hinges of the gates.

Inside the railing was Baba Yaga's hut, and it stood on hen's legs and walked about the yard. And in the yard there was standing Baba Yaga's servant, and she was crying bitterly because of the tasks Baba Yaga set her to do. She was crying bitterly and wiping her eyes on her petticoat.

Baba Yaga's hut stood on hen's legs and walked about the yard.

"How lucky," says the little girl, "that I picked up a handkerchief!" And she gave the handkerchief to Baba Yaga's servant, who wiped her eyes on it and smiled through her tears.

Close by the hut was a huge dog, very thin, gnawing a dry crust.

"How lucky," says the little girl, "that I picked up a loaf!" And she gave the loaf to the dog, and he gobbled it up and licked his lips.

The little girl went bravely up to the hut and knocked on the door.

"Come in," says Baba Yaga.

The little girl went in, and there was Baba Yaga, the bony-legged, the witch, sitting weaving at a loom. In a corner of the hut was a thin black cat watching a mouse-hole.

"Good-day to you, auntie," says the little girl, trying not to tremble.

"Good-day to you, niece," says Baba Yaga.

"My stepmother has sent me to you to ask for a needle and thread to mend a shirt."

"Very well," says Baba Yaga, smiling, and showing her iron teeth. "You sit down here at the loom, and go on with my weaving, while I go and get you the needle and thread."

The little girl sat down at the loom and began to weave.

Baba Yaga went out and called to her servant,

"Go, make the bath hot and scrub my niece. Scrub her clean. I'll make a dainty meal of her."

The servant came in for the jug. The little girl begged her, "Be not too quick in making the fire, and carry the water in a sieve." The servant smiled, but said nothing, because she was afraid of Baba Yaga. But she took a very long time about getting the bath ready.

Baba Yaga came to the window and asked,—

"Are you weaving, little niece? Are you weaving, my pretty?"

"I am weaving, auntie," says the little girl.

When Baba Yaga went away from the window, the little girl spoke to the thin black cat who was watching the mouse-hole.

"What are you doing, thin black cat?"

"Watching for a mouse," says the thin black cat. "I haven't had any dinner for three days."

"How lucky," says the little girl, "that I picked up the scraps of meat!" And she gave them to the thin black cat. The thin black cat gobbled them up, and said to the little girl,—

"Little girl, do you want to get out of this?"

"Catkin dear," says the little girl, "I do want to get out of this, for Baba Yaga is going to eat me with her iron teeth."

"Well," says the cat, "I will help you."

Just then Baba Yaga came to the window.

"Are you weaving, little niece?" she asked. "Are you weaving, my pretty?"

"I am weaving, auntie," says the little girl, working away, while the loom went clickety clack, clickety clack.

Baba Yaga went away.

Says the thin black cat to the little girl: "You have a comb in your hair, and you have a towel. Take them and run for it while Baba Yaga is in the bathhouse. When Baba Yaga chases after you, you must listen; and when she is close to you, throw away the towel, and it will turn into a big, wide river. It will take her a little time to get over that. But when she does, you must listen; and as soon as she is close to you throw away the comb, and it will sprout up into such a forest that she will never get through it at all."

"But she'll hear the loom stop," says the little girl.

"I'll see to that," says the thin black cat.

The cat took the little girl's place at the loom.

Clickety clack, clickety clack; the loom never stopped for a moment.

The little girl looked to see that Baba Yaga was in the bath-house, and then she jumped down from the little hut on hen's legs, and ran to the gates as fast as her legs could flicker.

The big dog leapt up to tear her to pieces. Just as he was going to spring on her he saw who she was.

"Why, this is the little girl who gave me the loaf," says he. "A good journey to you, little girl;" and he lay down again with his head between his paws.

When she came to the gates they opened quietly, quietly, without making any noise at all, because of the oil she had poured into their hinges.

Outside the gates there was a little birch tree that beat her in the eyes so that she could not go by.

"How lucky," says the little girl, "that I picked up the ribbon!" And she tied up the birch tree with the pretty blue ribbon. And the birch tree was so pleased with the ribbon that it stood still, admiring itself, and let the little girl go by.

How she did run!

Meanwhile the thin black cat sat at the loom. Clickety clack, clickety clack, sang the loom: but you never saw such a tangle as the tangle made by the thin black cat.

And presently Baba Yaga came to the window.

"Are you weaving, little niece?" she asked. "Are you weaving, my pretty?"

"I am weaving, auntie," says the thin black cat, tangling and tangling, while the loom went clickety clack, clickety clack.

"That's not the voice of my little dinner," says Baba Yaga, and she jumped into the hut, gnashing her iron teeth; and there was no little girl, but only the thin black cat, sitting at the loom, tangling and tangling the threads.

"Grr," says Baba Yaga, and jumps for the cat, and begins banging it about. "Why didn't you tear the little girl's eyes out?"

"In all the years I have served you," says the cat, "you have only given me one little bone; but the kind little girl gave me scraps of meat."

Baba Yaga threw the cat into a corner, and went out into the yard.

"Why didn't you squeak when she opened you?" she asked the gates.

"Why didn't you tear her to pieces?" she asked the dog.

"Why didn't you beat her in the face, and not let her go by?" she asked the birch tree.

"Why were you so long in getting the bath ready? If you had been quicker, she never would have got away," said Baba Yaga to the servant.

And she rushed about the yard, beating them all, and scolding at the top of her voice.

"Ah!" said the gates, "in all the years we have served you, you never even eased us with water; but the kind little girl poured good oil into our hinges."

"Ah!" said the dog, "in all the years I've served you, you never threw me anything but burnt crusts; but the kind little girl gave me a good loaf."

"Ah!" said the little birch tree, "in all the years I've served you, you never tied me up, even with thread; but the kind little girl tied me up with a gay blue ribbon."

"Ah!" said the servant, "in all the years I've served you, you have never given me even a rag; but the kind little girl gave me a pretty handkerchief."

Baba Yaga gnashed at them with her iron teeth. Then she jumped into the mortar and sat down. She drove it along with the pestle, and swept up her tracks with a besom, and flew off in pursuit of the little girl.

The little girl ran and ran. She put her ear to the ground and listened. Bang, bang, bangety bang! she could hear Baba Yaga beating the mortar with the pestle. Baba Yaga was quite close. There she was, beating with the pestle and sweeping with the besom, coming along the road.

As quickly as she could, the little girl took out the towel and threw it on the ground. And the towel grew bigger and bigger, and wetter and wetter, and there was a deep, broad river between Baba Yaga and the little girl.

The little girl turned and ran on. How she ran!

Baba Yaga came flying up in the mortar. But the mortar could not float in the river with Baba Yaga inside. She drove it in, but only got wet for her trouble. Tongs and pokers tumbling down a chimney are nothing to the noise she made as she gnashed her iron teeth. She turned home, and went flying back to the little hut on hen's legs. Then she got together all her cattle and drove them to the river.

"Drink, drink!" she screamed at them; and the cattle drank up all the river to the last drop. And Baba Yaga, sitting in the mortar, drove it with the pestle, and swept up her tracks with the besom, and flew over the dry bed of the river and on in pursuit of the little girl.

The little girl put her ear to the ground and listened. Bang, bang, bangety bang! She could hear Baba Yaga beating the mortar with the pestle. Nearer and nearer came the noise, and there was Baba Yaga, beating with the pestle and sweeping with the besom, coming along the road close behind.

The little girl threw down the comb, and it grew bigger and bigger, and its teeth sprouted up into a thick forest—so thick that not even Baba Yaga could force her way through. And Baba Yaga, gnashing her teeth and screaming with rage and disappointment, turned round and drove away home to her little hut on hen's legs.

The little girl ran on home. She was afraid to go in and see her stepmother, so she ran into the shed.

Scratch, scratch! Out came the little mouse.

"So you got away all right, my dear," says the little mouse. "Now run in. Don't be afraid. Your father is back, and you must tell him all about it."

The little girl went into the house.

"Where have you been?" says her father; "and why are you so out of breath?"

The stepmother turned yellow when she saw her, and her eyes glowed, and her teeth ground together until they broke.

But the little girl was not afraid, and she went to her father and climbed on his knee, and told him everything just as it had happened. And when the old man knew that the stepmother had sent his little daughter to be eaten by Baba Yaga, he was so angry that he drove her out of the hut, and ever afterwards lived alone with the little girl. Much better it was for both of them.

The little mouse came and lived in the hut, and every day it used to sit up on the table and eat crumbs, and warm its paws on the little girl's glass of tea.

The Little Daughter of the Snow

THERE WERE once an old man and an old woman, his wife, and they lived together in a hut, in a village on the edge of the forest. There were many people in the village; quite a town it was—eight huts at least, thirty or forty souls, good company to be had for crossing the road. But the old man and the old woman were unhappy, in spite of living like that in the very middle of the world.

All the other huts had babies in them—yes, and little ones playing about in the road outside, and having to be shouted at when any one came driving by. But there were no babies in their hut, and the old woman never had to go to the door to see where her little one had strayed to, because she had no little one.

And these two, the old man and the old woman, used to stand whole hours, just peeping through their window to watch the children playing outside. They had dogs and a cat, and cocks and hens, but none of these made up for having no children. These two would just stand and watch the children of the other huts. The dogs would bark, but they took no notice; and the cat would curl up against them, but they never felt her; and as for the cocks and hens, well, they were fed, but that was all. The old people did not care for them, and spent all their time in watching the children who belonged to the other huts.

In the winter the children in their little sheepskin coats played in the crisp snow. They pelted each other with snowballs, and shouted and laughed, and then they rolled the snow together and made a snow woman—a regular snow Baba Yaga, a snow witch; such an old fright!

And the old man, watching from the window, saw this, and he says to the old woman,—

"Wife, let us go into the yard behind and make a little snow girl; and perhaps she will come alive, and be a little daughter to us."

"Husband," says the old woman, "there's no knowing what may be. Let us go into the yard and make a little snow girl."

So the two old people put on their big coats and their fur hats, and went out into the yard, where nobody could see them.

And they rolled up the snow, and began to make a little snow girl. Very, very tenderly they rolled up the snow to make her little arms and legs. The good God helped the old people, and their little snow girl was more beautiful than ever you could imagine. She was lovelier than a birch tree in spring.

Well, towards evening she was finished—a little girl, all snow, with blind white eyes, and a little mouth, with snow lips tightly closed.

"Oh, speak to us," says the old man.

"Won't you run about like the others, little white pigeon?" says the old woman.

And she did, you know, she really did.

Suddenly, in the twilight, they saw her eyes shining blue like the sky on a clear day. And her lips flushed and opened, and she smiled. And there were her little white teeth. And look, she had black hair, and it stirred in the wind.

She began dancing in the snow, like a little white spirit, tossing her long hair, and laughing softly to herself.

Wildly she danced, like snowflakes whirled in the wind. Her eyes shone, and her hair flew round her, and she sang, while the old people watched and wondered, and thanked God.

This is what she sang:—

> "No warm blood in me doth glow,
>   Water in my veins doth flow;
>   Yet I'll laugh and sing and play
>   By frosty night and frosty day—
>   Little daughter of the Snow.

> "But whenever I do know
>   That you love me little, then
>   I shall melt away again.

She began dancing in the snow, like a little white spirit.

Back into the sky I'll go—
Little daughter of the Snow."

"God of mine, isn't she beautiful!" said the old
man. "Run, wife, and fetch a blanket to wrap her in
while you make clothes for her."

The old woman fetched a blanket, and put it
round the shoulders of the little snow girl. And the
old man picked her up, and she put her little cold
arms round his neck.

"You must not keep me too warm," she said.

Well, they took her into the hut, and she lay on a
bench in the corner farthest from the stove, while
the old woman made her a little coat.

The old man went out to buy a fur hat and boots
from a neighbour for the little girl. The neighbour
laughed at the old man; but a rouble is a rouble
everywhere, and no one turns it from the door, and
so he sold the old man a little fur hat, and a pair of
little red boots with fur round the tops.

Then they dressed the little snow girl.

"Too hot, too hot," said the little snow girl. "I
must go out into the cool night."

"But you must go to sleep now," said the old
woman.

"By frosty night and frosty day," sang the little
girl. "No; I will play by myself in the yard all night,
and in the morning I'll play in the road with the
children."

Nothing the old people said could change her mind.

"I am the little daughter of the Snow," she replied to everything, and she ran out into the yard into the snow.

How she danced and ran about in the moonlight on the white frozen snow!

The old people watched her and watched her. At last they went to bed; but more than once the old man got up in the night to make sure she was still there. And there she was, running about in the yard, chasing her shadow in the moonlight and throwing snowballs at the stars.

In the morning she came in, laughing, to have breakfast with the old people. She showed them how to make porridge for her, and that was very simple. They had only to take a piece of ice and crush it up in a little wooden bowl.

Then after breakfast she ran out in the road, to join the other children. And the old people watched her. Oh, proud they were, I can tell you, to see a little girl of their own out there playing in the road! They fairly longed for a sledge to come driving by, so that they could run out into the road and call to the little snow girl to be careful.

And the little snow girl played in the snow with the other children. How she played! She could run faster than any of them. Her little red boots flashed as she ran about. Not one of the other children was a match for her at snowballing. And when the children began making a snow woman, a Baba Yaga, you would have thought the little daughter of the Snow would have died of laughing. She laughed and laughed, like ringing peals on little glass bells. But she helped in the making of the snow woman, only laughing all the time.

When it was done, all the children threw snowballs at it, till it fell to pieces. And the little snow girl laughed and laughed, and was so quick she threw more snowballs than any of them.

The old man and the old woman watched her, and were very proud.

"She is all our own," said the old woman.

"Our little white pigeon," said the old man.

In the evening she had another bowl of ice-porridge, and then she went off again to play by herself in the yard.

"You'll be tired, my dear," says the old man.

"You'll sleep in the hut to-night, won't you, my love," says the old woman, "after running about all day long?"

But the little daughter of the Snow only laughed. "By frosty night and frosty day," she sang, and ran out of the door, laughing back at them with shining eyes.

And so it went on all through the winter. The little daughter of the Snow was singing and laughing and dancing all the time. She always ran out into the night and played by herself till dawn. Then she'd come in and have her ice-porridge. Then she'd play with the children. Then she'd have ice-porridge again, and off she would go, out into the night.

She was very good. She did everything the old woman told her. Only she would never sleep indoors. All the children of the village loved her. They did not know how they had ever played without her.

It went on so till just about this time of year. Perhaps it was a little earlier. Anyhow the snow was melting, and you could get about the paths. Often the children went together a little way into the forest in the sunny part of the day. The little snow girl went with them. It would have been no fun without her.

And then one day they went too far into the wood, and when they said they were going to turn back, little snow girl tossed her head under her little fur hat, and ran on laughing among the trees. The other children were afraid to follow her. It was getting dark. They waited as long as they dared, and then they ran home, holding each other's hands.

And there was the little daughter of the Snow out in the forest alone.

She looked back for the others, and could not see them. She climbed up into a tree; but the other trees were thick round her, and she could not see farther than when she was on the ground.

She called out from the tree,—

"Ai, ai, little friends, have pity on the little snow girl."

An old brown bear heard her, and came shambling up on his heavy paws.

"What are you crying about, little daughter of the Snow?"

"O big bear," says the little snow girl, "how can I help crying? I have lost my way, and dusk is falling, and all my little friends are gone."

"I will take you home," says the old brown bear.

"O big bear," says the little snow girl, "I am afraid of you. I think you would eat me. I would rather go home with some one else."

So the bear shambled away and left her.

An old gray wolf heard her, and came galloping up on his swift feet. He stood under the tree and asked,—

"What are you crying about, little daughter of the Snow?"

"O gray wolf," says the little snow girl, "how can I help crying? I have lost my way, and it is getting dark, and all my little friends are gone."

"I will take you home," says the old gray wolf.

"O gray wolf," says the little snow girl, "I am afraid of you. I think you would eat me. I would rather go home with some one else."

So the wolf galloped away and left her.

An old red fox heard her, and came running up to the tree on his little pads. He called out cheerfully, —

"What are you crying about, little daughter of the Snow?"

"O red fox," says the little snow girl, "how can I help crying? I have lost my way, and it is quite dark, and all my little friends are gone."

"I will take you home," says the old red fox.

"O red fox," says the little snow girl, "I am not afraid of you. I do not think you will eat me. I will go home with you, if you will take me."

So she scrambled down from the tree, and she held the fox by the hair of his back, and they ran together through the dark forest. Presently they saw the lights in the windows of the huts, and in a few minutes they were at the door of the hut that belonged to the old man and the old woman.

And there were the old man and the old woman, crying and lamenting.

"Oh, what has become of our little snow girl?"

"Oh, where is our little white pigeon?"

"Here I am," says the little snow girl. "The kind red fox has brought me home. You must shut up the dogs."

The old man shut up the dogs.

"We are very grateful to you," says he to the fox.

"Are you really?" says the old red fox; "for I am very hungry."

"Here is a nice crust for you," says the old woman.

"Oh," says the fox, "but what I would like would be a nice plump hen. After all, your little snow girl is worth a nice plump hen."

"Very well," says the old woman, but she grumbles to her husband.

"Husband," says she, "we have our little girl again."

"We have," says he; "thanks be for that."

"It seems waste to give away a good plump hen."

"It does," says he.

"Well, I was thinking," says the old woman, and then she tells him what she meant to do. And he went off and got two sacks.

In one sack they put a fine plump hen, and in the other they put the fiercest of the dogs. They took the bags outside and called to the fox. The old red fox came up to them, licking his lips, because he was so hungry.

They opened one sack, and out the hen fluttered. The old red fox was just going to seize her, when they opened the other sack, and out jumped the fierce dog. The poor fox saw his eyes flashing in the dark, and was so frightened that he ran all the way back into the deep forest, and never had the hen at all.

"That was well done," said the old man and the old woman. "We have got our little snow girl, and not had to give away our plump hen."

Then they heard the little snow girl singing in the hut. This is what she sang:—

> "Old ones, old ones, now I know
> Less you love me than a hen,
> I shall go away again.
> Good-bye, ancient ones, good-bye,
> Back I go across the sky;
> To my motherkin I go—
> Little daughter of the Snow."

They ran into the house. There were a little pool of water in front of the stove, and a fur hat, and a little coat, and little red boots were lying in it. And yet it seemed to the old man and the old woman that they saw the little snow girl, with her bright eyes and her long hair, dancing in the room.

"Do not go! do not go!" they begged, and already they could hardly see the little dancing girl.

But they heard her laughing, and they heard her song:—

> "Old ones, old ones, now I know
> Less you love me than a hen,
> I shall melt away again.
> To my motherkin I go—
> Little daughter of the Snow."

And just then the door blew open from the yard, and a cold wind filled the room, and the little daughter of the Snow was gone.

The little snow girl leapt into the arms of Frost her father and Snow her mother, and they carried her away over the stars to the far north, and there she plays all through the summer on the frozen seas. In winter she comes back to Russia, and some day, you know, when you are making a snow woman, you may find the little daughter of the Snow standing there instead.

Alenoushka and Her Brother

ONCE UPON a time there were two orphan children, a little boy and a little girl. Their father and mother were dead, and they were alone. The little boy was called Vanoushka,* and the little girl's name was Alenoushka.*

They set out together to walk through the whole of the great wide world. It was a long journey they set out on, and they did not think of any end to it, but only of moving on and on, and never stopping long enough in one place to be unhappy there.

They were travelling one day over a broad plain, padding along on their little bare feet. There were no trees on the plain, no bushes; open flat country as far as you could see, and the great sun up in the sky burning the grass and making their throats dry, and the sandy ground so hot that they could scarcely bear to set their feet on it. All day from early morning they had been walking, and the heat grew greater and greater towards noon.

*That means that they were called Ivan and Elena. Vanoushka and Alenoushka are affectionate forms of these names.

"Oh," said little Vanoushka, "my throat is so dry. I want a drink. I must have a drink—just a little drink of cool water."

"We must go on," said Alenoushka, "till we come to a well. Then we will drink."

They went on along the track, with their eyes burning and their throats as dry as sand on a stove.

But presently Vanoushka cried out joyfully. He saw a horse's hoofmark in the ground. And it was full of water, like a little well.

"Sister, sister," says he, "the horse has made a little well for me with his great hoof, and now we can have a drink; and oh, but I am thirsty!"

"Not yet, brother," says Alenoushka. "If you drink from the hoofmark of a horse, you will turn into a little foal, and that would never do."

"I am so very thirsty," says Vanoushka; but he did as his sister told him, and they walked on together under the burning sun.

A little farther on Vanoushka saw the hoofmark of a cow, and there was water in it glittering in the sun.

"Sister, sister," says Vanoushka, "the cow has made a little well for me, and now I can have a drink."

"Not yet, brother," says Alenoushka. "If you drink from the hoofmark of a cow, you will turn into a little calf, and that would never do. We must go on till we come to a well. There we will drink and rest ourselves. There will be trees by the well, and shadows, and we will lie down there by the quiet water and cool our hands and feet, and perhaps our eyes will stop burning."

So they went on farther along the track that scorched the bare soles of their feet, and under the sun that burned their heads and their little bare necks. The sun was high in the sky above them, and it seemed to Vanoushka that they would never come to the well.

But when they had walked on and on, and he was nearly crying with thirst, only that the sun had dried up all his tears and burnt them before they had time to come into his eyes, he saw another footprint. It was quite a tiny footprint, divided in the middle— the footprint of a sheep; and in it was a little drop of clear water, sparkling in the sun. He said nothing to his sister, nothing at all. But he went down on his hands and knees and drank that water, that little drop of clear water, to cool his burning throat. And he had no sooner drunk it than he had turned into a little lamb who ran round and round Alenoushka, frisking and leaping, with its little tail tossing in the air.

Alenoushka looked round for her brother, but could not see him. But there was the little lamb, leaping round her, trying to lick her face, and there in the ground was the print left by the sheep's foot.

She guessed at once what had happened, and

burst into tears. There was a hayrick close by, and under the hayrick Alenoushka sat down and wept. The little lamb, seeing her so sad, stood gravely in front of her; but not for long, for he was a little lamb, and he could not help himself. However sad he felt, he had to leap and frisk in the sun, and toss his little white tail.

Presently a fine gentleman came riding by on his big black horse. He stopped when he came to the hayrick. He was very much surprised at seeing a beautiful little girl sitting there, crying her eyes out, while a white lamb frisked this way and that, and played before her, and now and then ran up to her and licked the tears from her face with its little pink tongue.

"What is your name," says the fine gentleman, "and why are you in trouble? Perhaps I may be able to help you."

"My name is Alenoushka, and this is my little brother Vanoushka, whom I love." And she told him the whole story.

"Well, I can hardly believe all that," says the fine gentleman. "But come with me, and I will dress you in fine clothes, and set silver ornaments in your hair, and bracelets of gold on your little brown wrists. And as for the lamb, he shall come too, if you love him. Wherever you are there he shall be, and you shall never be parted from him."

And so Alenoushka took her little brother in her

arms, and the fine gentleman lifted them up before him on the big black horse, and galloped home with them across the plain to his big house not far from the river. And when he got home he made a feast and married Alenoushka, and they lived together so happily that good people rejoiced to see them, and bad ones were jealous. And the little lamb lived in the house, and never grew any bigger, but always frisked and played, and followed Alenoushka wherever she went.

And then one day, when the fine gentleman had ridden far away to the town to buy a new bracelet for Alenoushka, there came an old witch. Ugly she was, with only one tooth in her head, and wicked as ever went about the world doing evil to decent folk. She begged from Alenoushka, and said she was hungry, and Alenoushka begged her to share her dinner. And she put a spell in the wine that Alenoushka drank, so that Alenoushka fell ill, and before evening, when the fine gentleman came riding back, had become pale, pale as snow, and as thin as an old stick.

"My dear," says the fine gentleman, "what is the matter with you?"

"Perhaps I shall be better to-morrow," says Alenoushka.

Well, the next day the gentleman rode into the fields, and the old hag came again while he was out.

"Would you like me to cure you?" says she. "I

Ugly she was, with only one tooth in her head.

know a way to make you as well as ever you were. Plump you will be, and pretty again, before your husband comes riding home."

"And what must I do?" says Alenoushka, crying to think herself so ugly.

"You must go to the river and bathe this afternoon," says the old witch. "I will be there and put a spell on the water. Secretly you must go, for if any one knows whither you have gone my spell will not work."

So Alenoushka wrapped a shawl about her head, and slipped out of the house and went to the river. Only the little lamb, Vanoushka, knew where she had gone. He followed her, leaping about, and tossing his little white tail. The old witch was waiting for her. She sprang out of the bushes by the riverside, and seized Alenoushka, and tore off her pretty white dress, and fastened a heavy stone about her neck, and threw her from the bank into a deep place, so that she sank to the bottom of the river. Then the old witch, the wicked hag, put on Alenoushka's pretty white dress, and cast a spell, and made herself so like Alenoushka to look at that nobody could tell the difference. Only the little lamb had seen everything that had happened.

The fine gentleman came riding home in the evening, and he rejoiced when he saw his dear Alenoushka well again, with plump pink cheeks, and a smile on her rosy lips.

But the little lamb knew everything. He was sad and melancholy, and would not eat, and went every morning and every evening to the river, and there wandered about the banks, and cried, "Baa, baa," and was answered by the sighing of the wind in the long reeds.

The witch saw that the lamb went off by himself every morning and every evening. She watched where he went, and when she knew she began to hate the lamb; and she gave orders for the sticks to be cut, and the iron cauldron to be heated, and the steel knives made sharp. She sent a servant to catch the lamb; and she said to the fine gentleman, who thought all the time that she was Alenoushka, "It is time for the lamb to be killed, and made into a tasty stew."

The fine gentleman was astonished.

"What," says he, "you want to have the lamb killed? Why, you called it your brother when first I found you by the hayrick in the plain. You were always giving it caresses and sweet words. You loved it so much that I was sick of the sight of it, and now you give orders for its throat to be cut. Truly," says he, "the mind of woman is like the wind in summer."

The lamb ran away when he saw that the servant had come to catch him. He heard the sharpening of the knives, and had seen the cutting of the wood, and the great cauldron taken from its place. He was frightened, and he ran away, and came to the river bank, where the wind was sighing through the tall reeds. And there he sang a farewell song to his sister, thinking he had not long to live. The servant followed the lamb cunningly, and crept near to catch him, and heard his little song. This is what he sang:—

> "Alenoushka, little sister,
>   They are going to slaughter me;
>   They are cutting wooden fagots,
>   They are heating iron cauldrons,
>   They are sharpening knives of steel."

And Alenoushka, lamenting, answered the lamb from the bottom of the river:—

> "O my brother Ivanoushka,
>   A heavy stone is round my throat,
>   Silken grass grows through my fingers,
>   Yellow sand lies on my breast."

The servant listened, and marvelled at the miracle of the lamb singing, and the sweet voice answering him from the river. He crept away quietly, and came to the fine gentleman, and told him what he had heard; and they set out together to the river, to watch the lamb, and listen, and see what was happening.

The little white lamb stood on the bank of the river weeping, so that his tears fell into the water. And presently he sang again:—

"Alenoushka, little sister,
They are going to slaughter me;
They are cutting wooden fagots,
They are heating iron cauldrons,
They are sharpening knives of steel."

And Alenoushka answered him, lamenting, from the bottom of the river:—

"O my brother Ivanoushka,
A heavy stone is round my throat,
Silken grass grows through my fingers,
Yellow sand lies on my breast."

The fine gentleman heard, and he was sure that the voice was the voice of his own dear wife, and he remembered how she had loved the lamb. He sent his servant to fetch men, and fishing nets and nets of silk. The men came running, and they dragged the river with fishing nets, and brought their nets empty to land. Then they tried with nets of fine silk, and, as they drew them in, there was Alenoushka lying in the nets as if she were asleep.

They brought her to the bank and untied the stone from her white neck, and washed her in fresh water and clothed her in white clothes. But they had no sooner done all this than she woke up, more beautiful than ever she had been before, though then she was pretty enough, God knows. She woke, and sprang up, and threw her arms round the neck of the little white lamb, who suddenly became once more her little brother Vanoushka, who had been so thirsty as to drink water from the hoofmark of a sheep. And Vanoushka laughed and shouted in the sunshine, and the fine gentleman wept tears of joy. And they all praised God and kissed each other, and went home together, and began to live as happily as before, even more happily, because Vanoushka was no longer a lamb. But as soon as they got home the fine gentleman turned the old witch out of the house. And she became an ugly old hag, and went away to the deep woods, shrieking as she went.

Vanoushka grew up as handsome as Alenoushka was pretty. And he became a great hunter. And he married the sister of the fine gentleman. And they all lived happily together, and ate honey every day, with white bread and new milk.

The Fire-bird, the Horse of Power, and the Princess Vasilissa

ONCE UPON a time a strong and powerful Tzar ruled in a country far away. And among his servants was a young archer, and this archer had a horse—a horse of power—such a horse as belonged to the wonderful men of long ago—a great horse with a broad chest, eyes like fire, and hoofs of iron. There are no such horses nowadays. They sleep with the strong men who rode them, the bogatirs, until the time comes when Russia has need of them. Then the great horses will thunder up from under the ground, and the valiant men leap from the graves in the armour they have worn so long. The strong men will sit those horses of power, and there will be swinging of clubs and thunder of hoofs, and the earth will be swept clean from the enemies of God and the Tzar.

One day long ago, in the green time of the year, the young archer rode through the forest on his horse of power. The trees were green; there were little blue flowers on the ground under the trees;

71

the squirrels ran in the branches, and the hares in the undergrowth; but no birds sang. The young archer rode along the forest path and listened for the singing of the birds, but there was no singing. The forest was silent, and the only noises in it were the scratching of four-footed beasts, the dropping of fir cones, and the heavy stamping of the horse of power in the soft path.

"What has come to the birds?" said the young archer.

He had scarcely said this before he saw a big curving feather lying in the path before him. The feather was larger than a swan's, larger than an eagle's. It lay in the path, glittering like a flame; for the sun was on it, and it was a feather of pure gold. Then he knew why there was no singing in the forest. For he knew that the fire-bird had flown that way, and that the feather in the path before him was a feather from its burning breast.

The horse of power spoke and said,—

"Leave the golden feather where it lies. If you take it you will be sorry for it, and know the meaning of fear."

But the brave young archer sat on the horse of power and looked at the golden feather, and wondered whether to take it or not. He had no wish to learn what it was to be afraid, but he thought, "If I take it and bring it to the Tzar my master, he will be pleased; and he will not send me away with empty hands, for no tzar in the world has a feather from the burning breast of the fire-bird." And the more he thought, the more he wanted to carry the feather to the Tzar. And in the end he did not listen to the words of the horse of power. He leapt from the saddle, picked up the golden feather of the fire-bird, mounted his horse again, and galloped back through the green forest till he came to the palace of the Tzar.

He went into the palace, and bowed before the Tzar and said,—

"O Tzar, I have brought you a feather of the fire-bird."

The Tzar looked gladly at the feather, and then at the young archer.

"Thank you," says he; "but if you have brought me a feather of the fire-bird, you will be able to bring me the bird itself. I should like to see it. A feather is not a fit gift to bring to the Tzar. Bring the bird itself, or, I swear by my sword, your head shall no longer sit between your shoulders!"

The young archer bowed his head and went out. Bitterly he wept, for he knew now what it was to be afraid. He went out into the courtyard, where the horse of power was waiting for him, tossing its head and stamping on the ground.

"Master," says the horse of power, "why do you weep?"

"The Tzar has told me to bring him the fire-bird,

and no man on earth can do that," says the young archer, and he bowed his head on his breast.

"I told you," says the horse of power, "that if you took the feather you would learn the meaning of fear. Well, do not be frightened yet, and do not weep. The trouble is not now; the trouble lies before you. Go to the Tzar and ask him to have a hundred sacks of maize scattered over the open field, and let this be done at midnight."

The young archer went back into the palace and begged the Tzar for this, and the Tzar ordered that at midnight a hundred sacks of maize should be scattered in the open field.

Next morning, at the first redness in the sky, the young archer rode out on the horse of power, and came to the open field. The ground was scattered all over with maize. In the middle of the field stood a great oak with spreading boughs. The young archer leapt to the ground, took off the saddle, and let the horse of power loose to wander as he pleased about the field. Then he climbed up into the oak and hid himself among the green boughs.

The sky grew red and gold, and the sun rose. Suddenly there was a noise in the forest round the field. The trees shook and swayed, and almost fell. There was a mighty wind. The sea piled itself into waves with crests of foam, and the fire-bird came flying from the other side of the world. Huge and golden and flaming in the sun, it flew, dropped down with open wings into the field, and began to eat the maize.

The horse of power wandered in the field. This way he went, and that, but always he came a little nearer to the fire-bird. Nearer and nearer came the horse. He came close up to the fire-bird, and then suddenly stepped on one of its spreading fiery wings and pressed it heavily to the ground. The bird struggled, flapping mightily with its fiery wings, but it could not get away. The young archer slipped down from the tree, bound the fire-bird with three strong ropes, swung it on his back, saddled the horse, and rode to the palace of the Tzar.

The young archer stood before the Tzar, and his back was bent under the great weight of the fire-bird, and the broad wings of the bird hung on either side of him like fiery shields, and there was a trail of golden feathers on the floor. The young archer swung the magic bird to the foot of the throne before the Tzar; and the Tzar was glad, because since the beginning of the world no tzar had seen the fire-bird flung before him like a wild duck caught in a snare.

The Tzar looked at the fire-bird and laughed with pride. Then he lifted his eyes and looked at the young archer, and says he,—

"As you have known how to take the fire-bird, you will know how to bring me my bride, for whom I have long been waiting. In the land of Never, on

He came up close to the fire-bird, and then suddenly stepped on one of its spreading fiery wings.

the very edge of the world, where the red sun rises in flame from behind the sea, lives the Princess Vasilissa. I will marry none but her. Bring her to me, and I will reward you with silver and gold. But if you do not bring her, then, by my sword, your head will no longer sit between your shoulders!"

The young archer wept bitter tears, and went out into the courtyard, where the horse of power was stamping the ground with its hoofs of iron and tossing its thick mane.

"Master, why do you weep?" asked the horse of power.

"The Tzar has ordered me to go to the land of Never, and to bring back the Princess Vasilissa."

"Do not weep—do not grieve. The trouble is not yet; the trouble is to come. Go to the Tzar and ask him for a silver tent with a golden roof, and for all kinds of food and drink to take with us on the journey."

The young archer went in and asked the Tzar for this, and the Tzar gave him a silver tent with silver hangings and a gold-embroidered roof, and every kind of rich wine and the tastiest of foods.

Then the young archer mounted the horse of power and rode off to the land of Never. On and on he rode, many days and nights, and came at last to the edge of the world, where the red sun rises in flame from behind the deep blue sea.

On the shore of the sea the young archer reined in the horse of power, and the heavy hoofs of the horse sank in the sand. He shaded his eyes and looked out over the blue water, and there was the Princess Vasilissa in a little silver boat, rowing with golden oars.

The young archer rode back a little way to where the sand ended and the green world began. There he loosed the horse to wander where he pleased, and to feed on the green grass. Then on the edge of the shore, where the green grass ended and grew thin and the sand began, he set up the shining tent, with its silver hangings and its gold-embroidered roof. In the tent he set out the tasty dishes and the rich flagons of wine which the Tzar had given him, and he sat himself down in the tent and began to regale himself, while he waited for the Princess Vasilissa.

The Princess Vasilissa dipped her golden oars in the blue water, and the little silver boat moved lightly through the dancing waves. She sat in the little boat and looked over the blue sea to the edge of the world, and there, between the golden sand and the green earth, she saw the tent standing, silver and gold in the sun. She dipped her oars, and came nearer to see it the better. The nearer she came the fairer seemed the tent, and at last she rowed to the shore and grounded her little boat on the golden sand, and stepped out daintily and came up to the tent. She was a little frightened, and now and again she stopped and looked back to where the silver boat lay on the sand with the blue sea beyond it. The young archer said not a word, but went on regaling himself on the pleasant dishes he had set out there in the tent.

At last the Princess Vasilissa came up to the tent and looked in.

The young archer rose and bowed before her. Says he, —

"Good-day to you, Princess! Be so kind as to come in and take bread and salt with me, and taste my foreign wines."

And the Princess Vasilissa came into the tent and sat down with the young archer, and ate sweetmeats with him, and drank his health in a golden goblet of the wine the Tzar had given him. Now this wine was heavy, and the last drop from the goblet had no sooner trickled down her little slender throat than her eyes closed against her will, once, twice, and again.

"Ah me!" says the Princess, "it is as if the night itself had perched on my eyelids, and yet it is but noon."

And the golden goblet dropped to the ground from her little fingers, and she leant back on a cushion and fell instantly asleep. If she had been beautiful before, she was lovelier still when she lay in that deep sleep in the shadow of the tent.

Quickly the young archer called to the horse of power. Lightly he lifted the Princess in his strong young arms. Swiftly he leapt with her into the saddle. Like a feather she lay in the hollow of his left arm, and slept while the iron hoofs of the great horse thundered over the ground.

They came to the Tzar's palace, and the young archer leapt from the horse of power and carried the Princess into the palace. Great was the joy of the Tzar; but it did not last for long.

"Go, sound the trumpets for our wedding," he said to his servants; "let all the bells be rung."

The bells rang out and the trumpets sounded, and at the noise of the horns and the ringing of the bells the Princess Vasilissa woke up and looked about her.

"What is this ringing of bells," says she, "and this noise of trumpets? And where, oh, where is the blue sea, and my little silver boat with its golden oars?" And the Princess put her hand to her eyes.

"The blue sea is far away," says the Tzar, "and for your little silver boat I give you a golden throne. The trumpets sound for our wedding, and the bells are ringing for our joy."

But the Princess turned her face away from the Tzar; and there was no wonder in that, for he was old, and his eyes were not kind.

And she looked with love at the young archer; and there was no wonder in that either, for he was a young man fit to ride the horse of power.

The Tzar was angry with the Princess Vasilissa, but his anger was as useless as his joy.

"Why, Princess," says he, "will you not marry me, and forget your blue sea and your silver boat?"

"In the middle of the deep blue sea lies a great stone," says the Princess, "and under that stone is hidden my wedding dress. If I cannot wear that dress I will marry nobody at all."

Instantly the Tzar turned to the young archer, who was waiting before the throne.

"Ride swiftly back," says he, "to the land of Never, where the red sun rises in flame. There—do you hear what the Princess says?—a great stone lies in the middle of the sea. Under that stone is hidden her wedding dress. Ride swiftly. Bring back that dress, or, by my sword, your head shall no longer sit between your shoulders!"

The young archer wept bitter tears, and went out into the courtyard, where the horse of power was waiting for him, champing its golden bit.

"There is no way of escaping death this time," he said.

"Master, why do you weep?" asked the horse of power.

"The Tzar has ordered me to ride to the land of Never, to fetch the wedding dress of the Princess Vasilissa from the bottom of the deep blue sea. Besides, the dress is wanted for the Tzar's wedding, and I love the Princess myself."

"What did I tell you?" says the horse of power. "I told you that there would be trouble if you picked up the golden feather from the fire-bird's burning breast. Well, do not be afraid. The trouble is not yet; the trouble is to come. Up! into the saddle with you, and away for the wedding dress of the Princess Vasilissa!"

The young archer leapt into the saddle, and the horse of power, with his thundering hoofs, carried him swiftly through the green forests and over the bare plains, till they came to the edge of the world, to the land of Never, where the red sun rises in flame from behind the deep blue sea. There they rested, at the very edge of the sea.

The young archer looked sadly over the wide waters, but the horse of power tossed its mane and did not look at the sea, but on the shore. This way and that it looked, and saw at last a huge lobster moving slowly, sideways, along the golden sand.

Nearer and nearer came the lobster, and it was a giant among lobsters, the tzar of all the lobsters; and it moved slowly along the shore, while the horse of power moved carefully and as if by accident, until it stood between the lobster and the sea. Then, when the lobster came close by, the horse of power lifted an iron hoof and set it firmly on the lobster's tail.

"You will be the death of me!" screamed the lobster—as well he might, with the heavy foot of the horse of power pressing his tail into the sand. "Let me live, and I will do whatever you ask of me."

"Very well," says the horse of power; "we will let you live," and he slowly lifted his foot. "But this is what you shall do for us. In the middle of the blue sea lies a great stone, and under that stone is hidden the wedding dress of the Princess Vasilissa. Bring it here."

The lobster groaned with the pain in his tail. Then he cried out in a voice that could be heard all over the deep blue sea. And the sea was disturbed, and from all sides lobsters in thousands made their way towards the bank. And the huge lobster that was the oldest of them all and the tzar of all the lobsters that live between the rising and the setting of the sun, gave them the order and sent them back into the sea. And the young archer sat on the horse of power and waited.

After a little time the sea was disturbed again, and the lobsters in their thousands came to the shore, and with them they brought a golden casket in which was the wedding dress of the Princess Vasilissa. They had taken it from under the great stone that lay in the middle of the sea.

The tzar of all the lobsters raised himself painfully on his bruised tail and gave the casket into the hands of the young archer, and instantly the horse of power turned himself about and galloped back to the palace of the Tzar, far, far away, at the other side of the green forests and beyond the treeless plains.

The young archer went into the palace and gave the casket into the hands of the Princess, and looked at her with sadness in his eyes, and she looked at him with love. Then she went away into an inner chamber, and came back in her wedding dress, fairer than the spring itself. Great was the joy of the Tzar. The wedding feast was made ready, and the bells rang, and flags waved above the palace.

The Tzar held out his hand to the Princess, and looked at her with his old eyes. But she would not take his hand.

"No," says she; "I will marry nobody until the man who brought me here has done penance in boiling water."

Instantly the Tzar turned to his servants and ordered them to make a great fire, and to fill a great cauldron with water and set it on the fire, and, when the water should be at its hottest, to take the young archer and throw him into it, to do penance for having taken the Princess Vasilissa away from the land of Never.

There was no gratitude in the mind of that Tzar.

Swiftly the servants brought wood and made a mighty fire, and on it they laid a huge cauldron of water, and built the fire round the walls of the cauldron. The fire burned hot and the water steamed. The fire burned hotter, and the water bubbled and seethed. They made ready to take the young archer, to throw him into the cauldron.

"Oh, misery!" thought the young archer. "Why did I ever take the golden feather that had fallen from the fire-bird's burning breast? Why did I not listen to the wise words of the horse of power?" And he remembered the horse of power, and he begged the Tzar,—

"O lord Tzar, I do not complain. I shall presently die in the heat of the water on the fire. Suffer me, before I die, once more to see my horse."

"Let him see his horse," says the Princess.

"Very well," says the Tzar. "Say good-bye to your horse, for you will not ride him again. But let your farewells be short, for we are waiting."

The young archer crossed the courtyard and came to the horse of power, who was scraping the ground with his iron hoofs.

"Farewell, my horse of power," says the young archer. "I should have listened to your words of wisdom, for now the end is come, and we shall never more see the green trees pass above us and the ground disappear beneath us, as we race the wind between the earth and the sky."

"Why so?" says the horse of power.

"The Tzar has ordered that I am to be boiled to death—thrown into that cauldron that is seething on the great fire."

"Fear not," says the horse of power, "for the Princess Vasilissa has made him do this, and the end of these things is better than I thought. Go back, and when they are ready to throw you in the cauldron, do you run boldly and leap yourself into the boiling water."

The young archer went back across the courtyard, and the servants made ready to throw him into the cauldron.

"Are you sure that the water is boiling?" says the Princess Vasilissa.

"It bubbles and seethes," said the servants.

"Let me see for myself," says the Princess, and she went to the fire and waved her hand above the cauldron. And some say there was something in her hand, and some say there was not.

"It is boiling," says she, and the servants laid hands on the young archer; but he threw them from him, and ran and leapt boldly before them all into the very middle of the cauldron.

Twice he sank below the surface, borne round with the bubbles and foam of the boiling water. Then he leapt from the cauldron and stood before the Tzar and the Princess. He had become so beautiful a youth that all who saw cried aloud in wonder.

"This is a miracle," says the Tzar. And the Tzar looked at the beautiful young archer, and thought of himself—of his age, of his bent back, and his gray beard, and his toothless gums. "I too will become beautiful," thinks he, and he rose from his throne and clambered into the cauldron, and was boiled to death in a moment.

And the end of the story? They buried the Tzar, and made the young archer Tzar in his place. He married the Princess Vasilissa, and lived many years with her in love and good fellowship. And he built a golden stable for the horse of power, and never forgot what he owed to him.